The Absent-Minded Toad

by Javier Rondón

illustrations by Marcela Cabrera

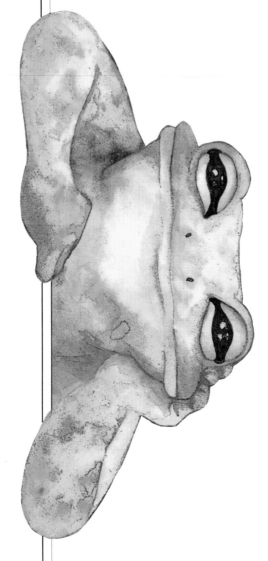

HARCOURT BRACE & COMPANY

Orlando   Atlanta   Austin   Boston   San Francisco   Chicago   Dallas   New York
Toronto   London

English translation copyright © 1994 by Harcourt Brace & Company
English translation by Kathryn Corbett

Grateful acknowledgment is made to Ediciones Ekaré, Caracas, Venezuela, for permission to reprint *The Absent-Minded Toad* by Javier Rondón, illustrated by Marcela Cabrera. © 1988 by Ediciones Ekaré. Originally published in Spanish under the title *El Sapo Distraído*.

Printed in the United States of America

ISBN 0-15-302121-7

4 5 6 7 8 9 10   035   97 96 95

A toad
of rainbow colors—
Orange, green,
and brown—

Made out a list

one morning

To take with him

to town.

Butter for tortillas,

Jam to put on toast.

He looked around his kitchen

For what he needed most.

A flower in his blue cap,

Around his leg a bell.

He smiled into his mirror.

He did look very well!

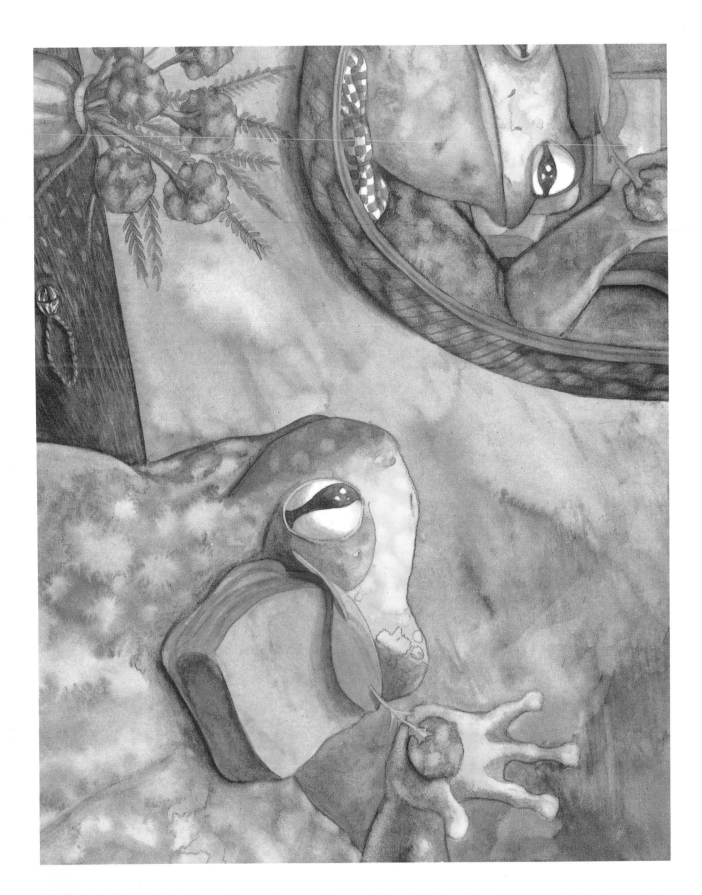

Then off he went to market—
Hop, hop, hop!
Looking in the windows
Of every kind of shop.

He stopped on the corner

Where the fruit seller sells

Fruits of many colors—

Oh, what lovely smells!

What a crowd of people
Dressed in their best!
Choosing cheese and brown eggs
Fresh from the nest.

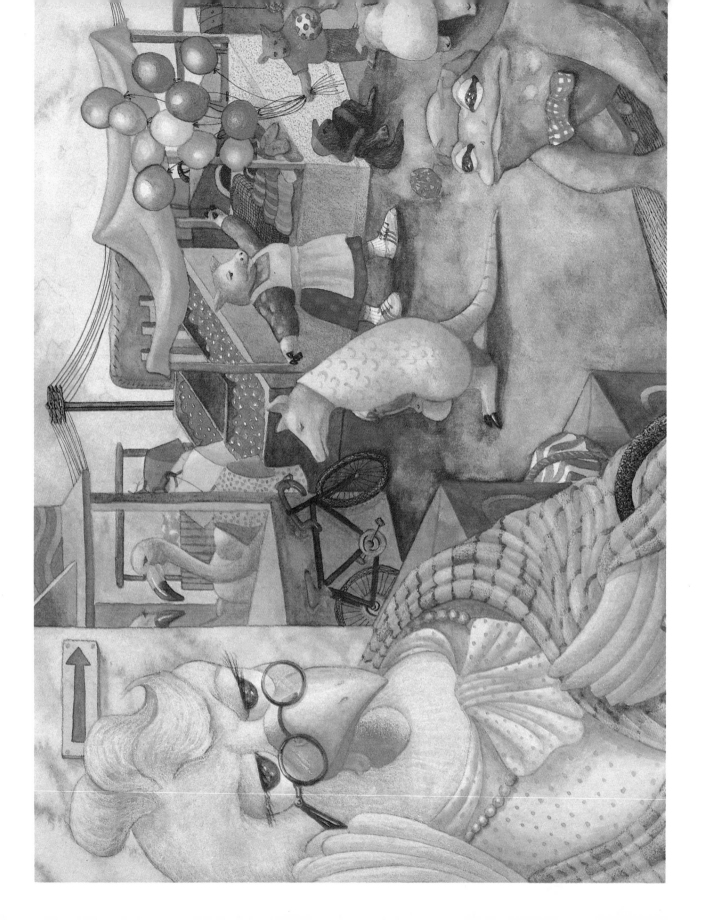

"Tomatoes from my garden!"
The tomato seller said.
"Here, lady, try one—
Fresh and ripe and red!"

The toad hopped round the market

Almost all the day.

In all that crowd of people

He nearly lost his way.

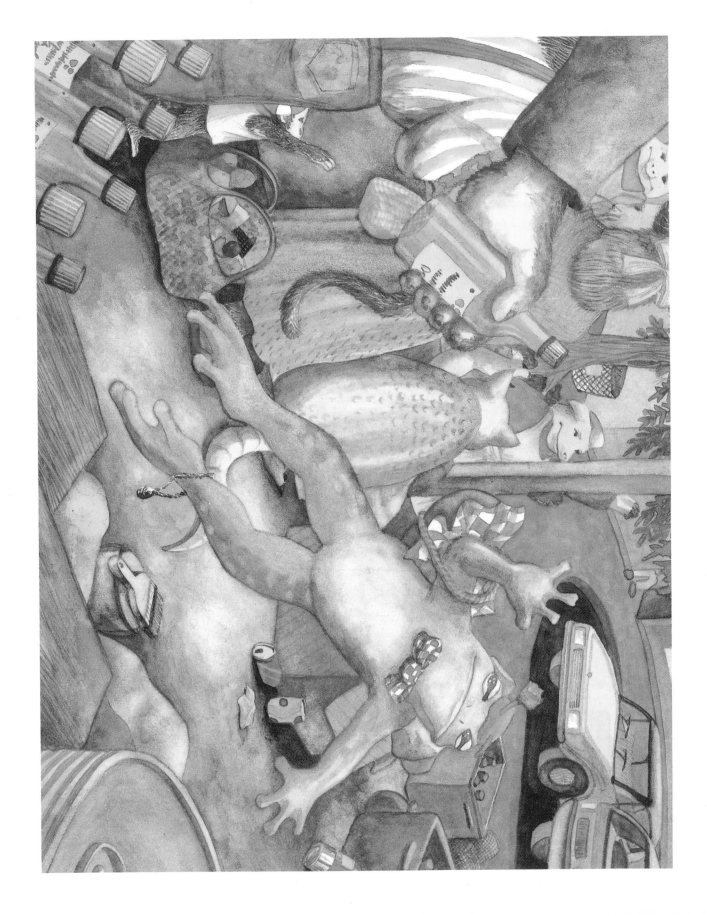

At last he got home safely
And put his feet up.
He drank some warm milk
From his old blue cup.

He went for bread and butter,

And then he said, "Oh, my!

I hopped all round the market,

But nothing did I buy!"